Alfie's Story

A true story

Love, Sue Wilkins.

— x —

Written by Sue Wilkins

Illustrated by Liz Furness

Bannister Publications Ltd

My name is Alfie. I'm a little black cat.
I think I'm cuddly, some say I'm fat.

A long time ago, when I was very small,
I had no one to love me, no one at all.

I had no name. I had no home.
I was so sad and all alone.

I searched for food wherever I could.
I slept in the hedgerow and sheltered in the wood.

Then one day, while wandering
around and about,
I saw a lady and heard her shout,

"Anna, Billy, it's time for tea"
I hid in her garden, as quiet as can be.

What happened next, well what a surprise,
I could hardly believe my very own eyes.

It was a tortoise-shell cat and
her black-and-white brother,
They raced to the lady,
playfully pushing each other.

Their tails were held high, their fur sleek and shiny,
I felt lost and afraid and oh, so tiny.

She spoke to them in a loving tone
And I knew, for sure, that this was their home.

They rushed into the house and ate food from a dish.
It smelled so delicious, I think it was fish.

Each day I would hide among the flowers
and listen and watch them for many hours.

They seemed so happy in their home together
and did not come out in nasty weather.

I was always hungry, often cold and wet
but then a day dawned I will never forget.

As I sat in the garden, beneath a tree,
I suddenly knew SHE was watching ME.

It was a beautiful, warm, sunny day.
I hoped she would not "shoo" me away.

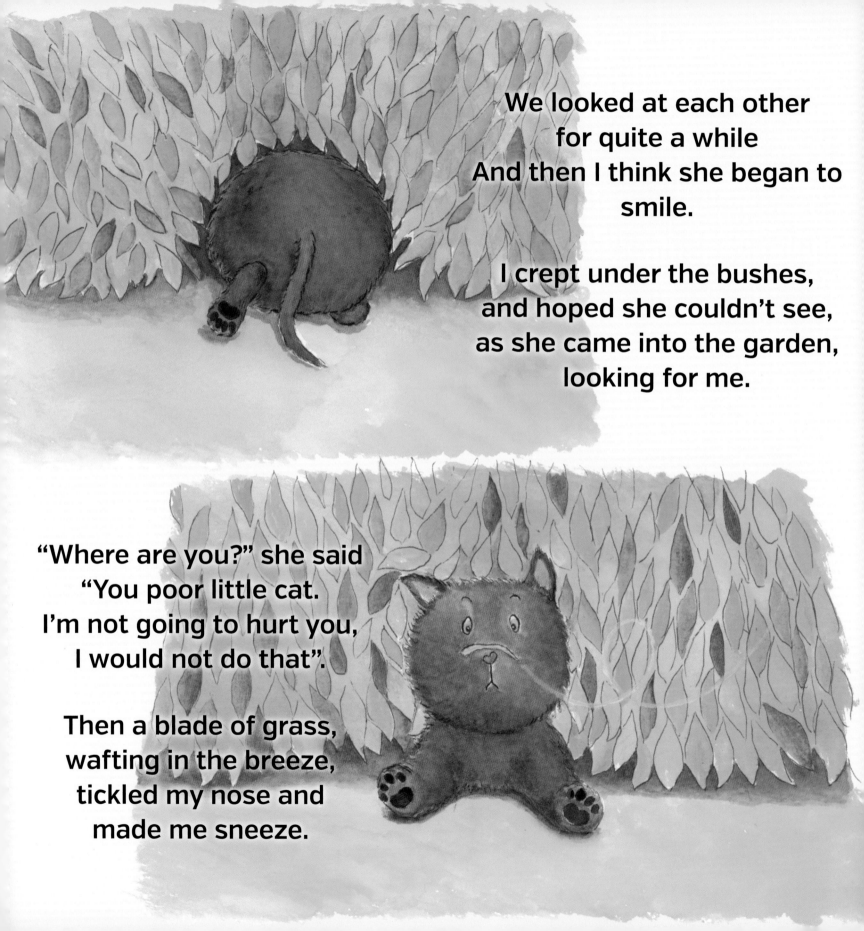

We looked at each other
for quite a while
And then I think she began to
smile.

I crept under the bushes,
and hoped she couldn't see,
as she came into the garden,
looking for me.

"Where are you?" she said
"You poor little cat.
I'm not going to hurt you,
I would not do that".

Then a blade of grass,
wafting in the breeze,
tickled my nose and
made me sneeze.

"Oh there you are, don't look so wary.
I'm really quite kind, not at all scary".

She did not come near, she knew I was lost
and even better, she did not seem cross.

"Oh dear", she said "You need something to eat",
and brought out, for me, a small plate of meat.

She placed the food on the ground, nearby,
but although I was hungry, I was timid and shy.

I felt safe where I sat, under the tree
and could not come out while she was watching me.

Then when I knew there was no-one around
I crept to the plate, without making a sound.

There was meat with gravy and biscuits too.
I began to think all my dreams had come true.

It was the best food I had ever tasted
and I knew not a scrap of it would be wasted

I licked the dish clean, then went back to a place
where I could secretly sit and wash my face.

I would sit beside the garden shed
when I was waiting to be fed.

But Winter was coming and the nights were getting cold
and as the days passed-by, I grew a little more bold.

One day as she placed my food in the shade,
I ran to the dish, I forgot to be afraid.

She stroked my back and
scratched my head,

"What a brave little cat",
she softly said.

And that was all, she truly
was kind,

when she stroked my back,
I did not mind.

In fact, I liked it very much,
she was warm and loving with
a gentle touch.

Then one very dark and
stormy night,
when the sky was black with
flashes of light.

There was grumbling, rumbling noise all around.
To a little cat, a fearful sound.

And then when the rain started tumbling down,
it was so heavy, I thought I would drown.

I ran to the house, where I could see a light,
squeezed onto the doorstep and "mewed" in fright.

As she opened the door, the wind howled in.
She saw me crouched there, soaked to the skin.

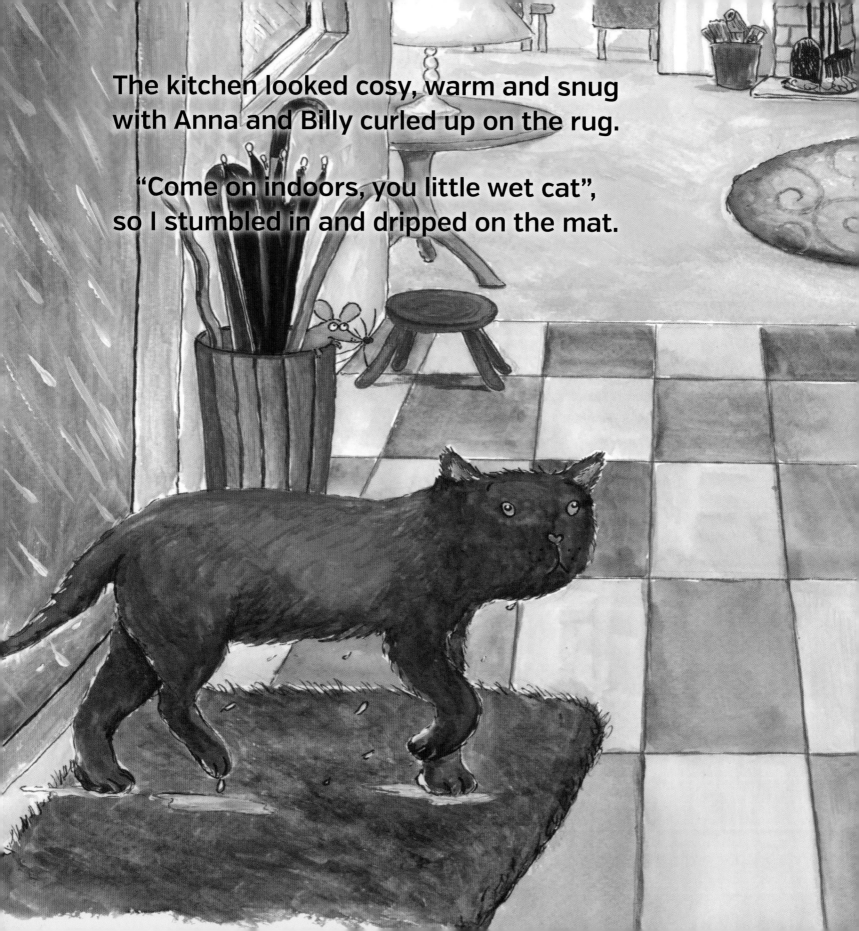

The kitchen looked cosy, warm and snug
with Anna and Billy curled up on the rug.

"Come on indoors, you little wet cat",
so I stumbled in and dripped on the mat.

My fur was matted, I was tired and scruffy
but she patted me dry with a towel, soft and fluffy.

I felt afraid as she closed the door.
I had never been in a house before.

To me, all this was very strange
and I crouched in the corner, by the range.

The lady looked at me and said "Goodnight",
as she locked the door and put out the light.

I listened and waited but it soon became clear
that there really was nothing for me to fear.

It was quiet and warm, my eyes were closing,
and before too long I was peacefully dozing.

I awoke to find that it was day and I had slept the
whole night away.

A shaft of sunlight shone across the floor
through a tiny window in the door.

Can you guess who stepped inside
as the little window opened wide?

It was Anna, who was closely followed by Billy.
They were prancing about and acting silly.

I soon knew why, it was easy to tell,
by the rattle of dishes and the wonderful smell.

It was breakfast time with milk and meat
and the three of us sat together to eat.

When Anna and Billy had eaten their fill,
they sat by the window, until

they must have seen something they could not ignore
because they suddenly rushed outside to explore.

That's when I learned something new,
something I could easily do.

The little window which was close to the floor
was not only a window but also a door.

They had pushed it open with paw and nose
and as they stepped through, it gently closed.

I nudged the little door with my head
and climbed through the opening onto the step.

Then just to be sure I knew what to do,
I pushed it again and climbed back through.

I thought I must be a lucky black cat
as I sat in the warmth on the mat.

I had a bed of my own and food aplenty
which meant my tummy would never be empty.

Now I have no need to roam,
I know I'm loved and have a happy home.

But best of all, when it's time for tea,
She now calls, "Anna, Billy and Alfie".

First published in Great Britain in 2014 and reprinted in 2015 and 2018 by

Bannister Publications Ltd
118 Saltergate
Chesterfield
Derbyshire S40 1NG

ISBN 978-1-909813-05-2

Designed by Escritor Design, Chesterfield, Derbyshire
Printed and bound in Great Britain by SRP Ltd
Exeter, Devon

bannister●
publications